# SOCCER SCOOP

THE #1
SPORTS SERIES
FOR KIDS

# SOCCER SCOOP

LITTLE, BROWN AND COMPANY
Books for Young Readers
New York   Boston

Little, Brown Books for Young Readers

Hachette Book Group
237 Park Avenue, New York, NY 10017
Visit our Web site at www.lb-kids.com

www.mattchristopher.com

Little, Brown Books for Young Readers is a division of Hachette Book Group, Inc. The Little, Brown name and logo are trademarks of Hachette Book Group, Inc.

First Paperback Edition: January 1998

Library of Congress Cataloging-in-Publication Data

Christopher, Matt.
   Soccer scoop / Matt Christopher. — 1st ed.
      P.     cm.
   Summary: When a cartoon appears in the school newspaper
making fun if his tendency to talk a lot, Mac, the goalie for
the cougars soccer team, is determined to find out who is
responsible.
      ISBN 978-0-316-14206-9 (hc) / ISBN 978-0-316-18896-8 (pb)
      [1. Soccer — Fiction.       2. Schools— Fiction.]
1. Title.
PZ7.C458So   1998
[Fic] — dc21

                                                         97-24455

            20  19  18  17  16  15  14  13  12  11

                         COM-MO

            Printed in the United States of America

# SOCCER SCOOP

**L**ate afternoon sunlight streamed through the trees at the far end of the field. The game between the Cornwall Cougars and the Bristol Knights was winding down. Tired from a hard-fought game, the teams were playing a little sloppily. One penalty after another was called as the Knights tried to get a goal on the scoreboard. At the moment, however, it read, Cougars 3, Knights 0.

Watching the action from his position at the Cougars' goal, Mac Williams danced back and forth. The rapid motion helped to keep him warm. It also kept his reflexes active. He never knew when the play would turn around. In an instant, there could be a thundering horde of players stampeding their way toward one spot — the twenty-four-by-eight-foot gap that marked the opening to the goal.

As he bounced back and forth, Mac kept up a stream of commentary.

"Come on, you Cougars! Let's go, Mickey! Nice trap, Dougie! Oh my gosh, oh my gosh, Mel, there's a hole! Fill it in, fill it in! Way to go! Yes! Where's the ball, where is it? Right on, Jackie. Okay, you guys, here they come. I'm ready for you! Way to go, Cougars — took it away from them!"

Mac was a top-notch goalie, but that wasn't his only claim to fame. He was just as well known for his way with words — and he used them a lot!

Even at his distance, Mac could see the action taking place at the opposite end of the field. He watched as his teammates set up a play that could bring them yet another goal. But left wing Stevie Fisk's pass to Mac's best friend, Dougie Cooper, just missed its mark. It glanced against his heel and went sailing across the field.

"All right, Dougie, eye on the ball — foot on it, too! Oh, not so fast, Mr. Knight Wing. Missed your chance, didn't you?"

There was a burst of laughter in the stands. Some of the Cougar fans could hear Mac loud and clear. His chatter never really stopped, but it did slow down when the play was near the goal.

It looked as though that was about to happen.

With less than a minute to go, the Knights had managed to wrest the ball from the Cougars and race it downfield into Cougar territory. Only a few defenders were positioned to hold them off.

As the Knights set up a play for a goal shot, their sole obstacle was Mac. Luckily for the Cougars, the Knights had no idea how serious an obstacle he was.

The Knights had tried this same play in their first attempt for a goal. That's all Mac needed. The play was fixed in his memory, and he was ready for them.

As the Knight wing swept by the front of the goal, he kicked a short pass upfield and a little behind him. A Knight coming from the opposite side of the field broke away from his blocker. He positioned himself and booted the ball cross-corner toward the net.

Mac had been covering the middle, but as soon as he saw the setup, he leaped into position, arms outspread — and made the block! The ball dropped at his feet. He gathered it in his hands, surveyed the field, then booted it toward the opposite goal.

The crowd roared its approval.

"Mac! Mac! Mac!" and "Defense!" could be heard amid applause and the shouts for the Cougars. On an impulse, Mac glanced over in that direction and gave the fans a little wave.

The cheering simply got louder. Before Mac turned his attention back to the action, he noticed that Jimmy Palumbo, the sports editor of the *Cornwall Chronicle*, the school newspaper, was on his feet, leading the cheers in the stands.

Jimmy was new in town, though Mac and the other Cougars had already known him by reputation. He had been the lead scorer for one of the Cougars' rivals, the Henryville Hornets, the year before. And he would have made the Cougars squad this year, but at the beginning of the summer, Jimmy was in a bad car accident. The driver had been thrown free, but one of Jimmy's legs had been broken.

Jimmy wasn't on crutches anymore, but there was no way that he was going to play soccer this season. Mac had heard that he had asked Coach Robertson if he could help out on the coaching side of things. But apparently Coach Robertson had turned him down, saying he had more than enough help on the sidelines. In the end, Jimmy opted to report on the weekly games for the school paper.

Poor Jimmy, Mac thought. I think I'd go nuts if I couldn't play soccer!

On the field, the action had reversed itself in an instant. A breakaway ball skittered down to Cougar territory. The captain of the Knights raced for it with incredible speed for someone who had played the whole game.

Billy Levine, the team's sweeper, tried to take the ball from him. But he slipped in the mud and went down.

Now the Knight was all alone in front of the net. Only Mac would stand in his way when it came time for his shot.

Adrenaline shot through Mac's system. He had no way of knowing where the Knight was going to aim. Then, suddenly, the ball was sailing through the air. It looked as though it was going to go in and spoil the shutout.

But even though he had only a few seconds to react, Mac's energy gave him the extra inches he needed. With outstretched hands, he just managed to deflect the ball and prevent the goal.

At that very second, the final whistle blew, signaling the end of the game.

# 2

**A**s usual after a victory, the Cougars' locker room was noisy with the sounds of celebration. As the players cleaned up and packed their gear, they congratulated each other on a game well played. Mac was his usual vocal self, commenting on just about every major play of the game. He had good words to say for everyone who had done well, including a generous measure of self-praise for his own efforts.

"Thought they had me on that last one, didn't they?" he asked Mickey Davies, a tall, thin regular on the forward line. Before

Mickey could open his mouth, Mac supplied the answer: "Gotta get up pretty early in the day to put one by Big Mac!"

Mickey just shook his head and moved on.

"Speaking of which, what do you say, Dougie? Want to celebrate with a burger and a milk shake? I'll let you buy," Mac said. "I figure you owe me because of that pass you missed just near the end of the game."

"Considering the fact that my two goals helped win the game, *you* might think about buying *me* a milk shake and burger — and fries to go with it," said Dougie Cooper.

"Oh, yeah? Don't you think you'd better lay off the grub for a while? You're starting to look kind of chunky and slow out there, buddy."

Dougie and Mac had been friends since kindergarten. Both were good athletes, and both loved playing soccer. Dougie had incredible speed and was a natural for the front line. Mac, built taller and wider, had a solid presence as a goalie. Since they never competed with each other for a spot on the team, they could exchange good-natured banter without hurting each other.

The coach understood this and let them blow off steam at each other. After all, it was harmless. But not everyone else understood. Sometimes the other guys seemed turned off by the way Mac and Dougie went on. Billy Levine, the team's burly defensive sweeper, even now was rolling his eyes.

"You guys really take the cake, you know?" he said. "Don't you know it took the whole team to win the game?"

"No, really?" asked Mac, faking surprise. "You mean I'm not the Cougars' only defense? You could have fooled me!" He looked at Billy slyly. "Say, think you could teach me that move you did at the end of the game? You know, the one where you end up gazing at the sky while the opposite team dribbles by you? Do you think the mud on the backside of your uniform will ever come clean?"

Billy reddened and opened his mouth for a retort when a new face appeared in the locker room.

"What's this, fighting in the ranks?" shouted Jimmy Palumbo. He was edging his way among the benches and soggy-haired players. Pausing at the far wall, where Mac and Dougie were stuffing their gear into their duffels, he pushed aside a towel and sat down on a bench. "Better watch out or I'll be forced to report that trouble was brewing in the locker room."

"Ah, Jimmy 'Scoop' Palumbo enters the scene," said Mac. "Maybe you'd like to spring for a couple of milk shakes while you pump us for quotes."

"Sure, why not?" said Jimmy. "You can tell

me what it was like in kindergarten around here."

"When Mac defended the sandbox from all attackers," Dougie joked. "And then told all the teachers what a swell job he'd done."

"You mean he was playing to the crowd even back then?" asked Jimmy.

"Hey, I could tell you stories," said Dougie. "Remember, I knew this guy when he was barely out of diapers."

"Yeah, and you were still wearing them," said Mac.

That brought laughter to the rest of the group in the locker room. Even Billy Levine cracked a smile.

"Come on, Jimmy. You, too, Dougie," Mac went on. "And anyone else who wants to come along. I'll buy. It's the only way I'll end up getting some myself."

"And the only way you'll get us to listen to your early war stories," said Dougie.

"Hey, I got a million of 'em!" said Mac, smiling.

As a small group lined up behind him, there was general agreement that he was right about that!

# 3

When Mac got on the school bus Monday morning, he was still in great spirits. The Cougars were well on their way to a winning season, and he was playing at his best.

The return trip at the end of the day was the exact opposite. He was in a dark, angry mood and could barely think about the Cougars.

What had happened to cause such a shift?

All day long, Mac had shared his buoyant feelings with his classmates. It seemed as though he was the unofficial school cheerleader.

When Dougie solved a difficult problem in math class, Mac was heard to mumble, "Way to go, Einstein!"

When the results of the previous week's special U.S. history contest were posted on the bulletin board, he noted the names of a few Cougars on the list with, "Well, at least some of us know what's been going on in this country!"

And when he missed an easy word in the semifinals of the weekly spelling contest, he mocked himself by saying, "As you can see, words fail me!" Then he laughed with everyone else when someone yelled back, "Well, that's a first!"

On top of all that, he was greeted cheerfully by just about everyone in the school building. It seemed as though they all knew that he had played well in the game against the Knights.

"Nice game you had yesterday," said Mr. Sullivan, the head custodian. Mac was waiting for him to finish tightening a connection on the watercooler.

"Were you there? Did you watch the game?" Mac asked, bending over to sip the icy liquid.

"No, but I heard about it," said Mr. Sullivan. "Whole school's talking about how well the Cougars are playing this year. I even read all about it in the Palumbo boy's column."

"Best season ever, so far," Mac said, wiping his lips with the back of his hand.

"Uh-huh," Mr. Sullivan said, nodding. "Lots of talk about you, too. You're playing real well, they say."

"Well, I'm glad somebody notices," said Mac with a big smile.

"Oh, they notice," said Mr. Sullivan. "They notice a lot of things."

"Like what else?" Mac asked, suddenly curious.

Mr. Sullivan just smiled, picked up his

toolbox, and lumbered down the corridor.

Mac shrugged. He couldn't imagine what sort of "things" Mr. Sullivan had in mind.

He found out when he was on his way to practice that afternoon. Outside the school building, copies of the *Cornwall Chronicle* were being handed out. He took one and was about to stuff it into his duffel when Dougie grabbed his arm.

"You're okay, aren't you?" he asked.

"Of course I am," Mac replied. "Why wouldn't I be? What's the matter?"

Dougie pointed at the newspaper. "You haven't seen it, then, have you?"

"What are you talking about?" Mac asked. "Jimmy's column? Didn't he say I played a great game?"

"Of course he did, but . . . oh, boy!" said Dougie. "There's a new cartoon, and you'd better take a look at it right now."

He pulled Mac off to one side and opened the paper to the midsection. The two-page

17

spread contained its usual display of school photographs — but there was something new. In the center was a hand-drawn cartoon.

It showed the goal section of a soccer field. The goalie, whose head consisted of just a mouth and two eyes, was leaning up against the post. He was waving to the crowd while a stream of sentences poured out of his mouth. All around him, other soccer players were pictured drowning in the sea of words. One player was calling out, "Man over-bored!" and reaching for a life preserver with the word *silence* written on it.

The caption beneath the cartoon read, *Motor Mouth: It never runs out of gas (though some wish it would)!*

The drawing was pretty rough. But there was no doubt about who it was meant to be.

And that person didn't think it was at all funny.

**4**

**M**ac stared at the cartoon, then looked at Dougie.

Dougie tried to smile. "It's just a joke, you know. Somebody's idea of being funny."

"So how come I'm not laughing?" asked Mac. "Someone's making me look stupid, and I want to know who it is."

"How are you going to find out? There's no credit for the cartoon," asked Dougie.

"I'm going to ask Jimmy. After all, he's the sports editor," said Mac. "He ought to know."

"Look, I don't think you should get all bent out of shape over this. It's some smart

19

aleck's dumb sense of humor. Everyone will laugh for a minute and then forget it," said Dougie.

"Well, maybe," said Mac reluctantly. "But I'm still going to talk to Jimmy."

"Hey, don't you think there's something you ought to do first?" asked Dougie.

Mac gave him a blank stare.

"Practice! Come on, we're already a few minutes late."

They raced into the locker room and quickly changed into their practice gear. A few seconds later, they were on the field, where the warm-up had already begun. The rest of their teammates were starting their stretching exercises as Mac and Dougie hurried to catch up to them.

Mac settled into the goal spot, ready to begin a scrimmage.

"Okay, boys, let's see some action out there! Let's see if you can get one by me today! Betcha can't, betcha can't!"

At first, Mac didn't notice the snickering. Then he heard someone make a revving motor sound and saw everyone look over at him and laugh.

"What's that all about?" Mac asked Billy Levine, who had stopped to lace up his cleat next to the net.

"Don't you read the paper?" Billy called back as he raced back to his position.

Mac stomped back and forth between the goalposts.

Dougie is wrong, he said to himself. Everyone saw the cartoon, and they think it's okay to make fun of me. Well, it's not. He sighed and shook his head. But today, I'll let my playing do the talking!

He clapped his gloved hands together and flexed his knees. He was ready for whatever came his way.

In this case, it was the faster group of players, who came bearing down on the goal. Jackie Hamlin, the right wing, had no trouble dribbling the ball around Billy, the sweeper. Mac had to bite his tongue to keep from calling out for Billy to pay better attention. Luckily a crowd of players kept getting in front of Jackie's line to the goal.

Finally Mac could tell by the expression on Jackie's face that he was about to take his shot. Reading the offense like that was one of the things that made Mac a terrific goaltender.

Sure enough, despite the awkward angle, Jackie booted the ball in the direction of the net.

Mac was ready at the far corner, even though there wasn't a chance the ball would go in. As it came his way, he moved forward and scooped it up. Then, scanning the field, he saw a big gap to the far left. Quickly positioning his body, he punted the ball toward that part of the field.

"I can read you like a book, Jackie!" he yelled out. "You may be able to get by my sweeper with no trouble, but you can't put one by me!"

Just then the whistle blew. The coach sent in some substitutes and switched a few players around.

"Nice save," he heard Billy Levine say on his way to the sidelines.

"Thanks," said Mac. "You know, if you had kept a little more to the left when Jackie brought the ball downfield, he might not have gotten by you so easily."

Billy frowned. "Yeah, well, I'll try to re-member that next time, *Coach*," he said sar-castically.

Mac shrugged. If Billy couldn't take some constructive criticism, it was no big deal to him. Just so long as he didn't make things harder for Mac.

For the rest of the day's practice, it was soccer as usual. By the time they were head-ing for the locker room, Mac had convinced himself that Dougie was right. The guff he'd gotten because of the silly cartoon would all blow over soon enough.

After the coach finished his rundown on that day's practice, he reminded everyone that the Cougars' next game was that Friday against the league-leading Bakersville Bruins. He wanted everyone playing at their peak form — and no nonsense about that.

What did he mean about "no nonsense"? Mac wondered after the coach left. Of course everyone would play their best.

**5**

**T**hat's when the silliness broke out in the locker room. Marv Daley, a beefy midfielder, climbed up on a bench and started reciting, "Friends, Romans, and countrymen, let me tell you about how great I am at this game." Then he made a sound like a sputtering motor. Everyone in the locker room broke out into laughter. Mel Walters, the tallest member of the team, was doubled over in mirth. Everyone except Mac. The color rose in his face as his blood boiled inside.

Dougie poked him in the ribs and whispered, "Come on, it's just a joke."

Mac glanced at him, knowing that Dougie

was right. He knew he had to do something to prove he could take it.

He jumped up on the bench, and, copying Marv's pose, he shouted, "Don't shoot until you see the whites of their goalie's eyes! And if I have but one soccer game to win, let it be against the Bruins!"

The laughter turned to cheers. Several of the players came by and exchanged high fives with Mac. By the time the place had cleared out, there wasn't a trace of ridicule left.

But deep down inside, Mac was stinging from the barb that had been thrown at him. That's why he was moody when he boarded the late-afternoon-activities bus. He had a feeling that the newspaper cartoon might not be just a one-shot thing. Someone was trying to make a fool of him; he was convinced.

That evening, right after dinner, he called Jimmy.

"Okay, buddy, time to tell all," he said into

the phone. "Who's the new cartoonist of the *Chronicle*'s sports department?"

"The *Chronicle* has someone new doing cartoons, sure," said Jimmy. "But I don't know who it is."

"What do you mean? That was a sports cartoon that ran in this week's paper, wasn't it?" Mac said. "And you're the sports editor, so you must know!"

"Hey, cool it," said Jimmy. "I'm telling you, I don't know who did that cartoon. No one talked to me about it, so I wasn't all that happy, either, you know? I mean, like you said, I'm the sports editor, so I figured that stuff should come through me. I asked around and discovered that the paper's editor, Margie Lewis, isn't talking. She's keeping it a big secret. Claims 'journalistic privilege' or something like that. Anyhow, I knew you wouldn't like it as soon as I saw it, so I did my best to find out something. But I hit a stone wall."

"Not even a clue?" asked Mac.

"Nope," said Jimmy. "Zilch."

"Think I'd get anywhere if I asked Margie?" Mac said.

"Nope," said Jimmy. "I don't think anyone will. Maybe it's best to just drop it."

"All right," said Mac. "Thanks, Jimmy. G'bye."

But just the way his tongue wouldn't leave a sore tooth alone, his thoughts kept going back to the picture of Motor Mouth.

For the rest of the week, Mac practiced hard — but he was a lot quieter down in the goal area. He was just as effective in the goal as before, but the old zip seemed to be missing a little.

After Thursday's final practice before the Bruins game, Coach Robertson beckoned to him to come and see him.

"Something on your mind, Mac?" asked the coach.

"No, sir," said Mac.

The coach looked at him for a long moment. "Mac, you're the best goalie I've ever had on a team I've coached."

Mac's heart leaped with pride at those words —

"But . . ."

— and then sank at that tone.

"But what?" he asked the coach.

"Well, I've come to expect even more out of you. I've watched you size up the play on the field, and your instincts are terrific. What you pick up could be a lot of help to all of us."

"You mean you listen to what I say?"

"Well," said the coach, smiling, "it's a little like driving with the car radio playing an all-news station. Sometimes you tune in; sometimes you don't. But I listen to enough to know that if you ever got injured and couldn't play, I'd have you on the sidelines feeding me information."

"Like one of your assistant coaches?" asked Mac incredulously.

"Something like that," said Coach Robertson. "It's a valuable player who can combine ability with knowledge. And I'd like you to feel free to share that knowledge with me."

Mac stared at him, wide-eyed.

"So, if there's something bothering you," the coach went on, "get rid of it. Get it out of your system, and get out there and play the game — the whole game — you're capable of."

Swelling with pride, Mac left the coach's office.

On the bus ride home, Mac slid into a seat with Dougie. Jimmy, who had stayed after to help out with the newspaper, was in the seat in front of them.

"Guess what happened after practice?" Mac said. He told the two boys about his conversation with the coach. "Can you believe that? He was practically asking me to be part of his sideline team!"

"Jeez, when *I* asked him at the beginning of the season if I could help out like that, he said he didn't need anyone else," Jimmy mumbled.

Mac and Dougie exchanged looks. "Hey, Jimmy, I'm sure he only asked me because I've been playing for him for two years now," Mac said reassuringly. "He knows what I can do. He only knew about you through last year's sports columns and when we played your team. And besides, I don't plan on getting injured anytime soon. So his offer isn't likely to be accepted anyhow, right?"

Jimmy shrugged. "I guess so." Then he grinned. "Maybe I should stop being so complimentary to you in my articles. Seems like you need to be taken down a notch, not boosted up!"

**6**

By game time on Friday, the newspaper cartoon had receded to the furthest reaches of Mac's mind. He was determined to play his best against the Bruins, especially when it came to reading their plays. In fact, he was going to speak up about everything he noticed, no matter which team was doing what. After all, the coach himself said that helped, right?

Mac looked around him at the field of players in their Cougars yellow-and-black uniforms. They showed every bit as much vigor as the front-running Bruins in their dark brown uniforms with the silver trim. He just hoped that yellow would triumph over brown that day.

In less than a minute after the game had begun, he could tell it was going to be one tough battle. The Bruins controlled the ball the entire time and brought it within range of the goal more than once.

"Defense!" Mac called out to his team-mates. "Come on, Billy, dig in! Right wing! Right wing! All by himself! Cover him, Mickey! Way to go!"

Mac moved back and forth, side to side. Sometimes he moved far forward. Even though leaving the net was a little risky, he had learned that doing so made it look to the opposing offense as though he filled up more of the goal. With an apparently limited net area to shoot for, more than one Bruin seemed to change his mind about a goal attempt.

Not that that stopped them completely.

But after two failed attempts, the Bruins' offense lost the ball to the Cougars. Unfortunately Mac could see that Dougie and Jackie were having their troubles setting up goal attempts. The Bruins hadn't gotten to the number one slot by luck. They had a solid defense and used it well.

When the Bruins' goalie picked off a loose ball that came within his range, he booted it downfield to move the play back to Mac's side of the field.

A sea of brown-and-silver bodies seemed to swarm in front of him all at once, with little protection from the wearers of yellow and black.

"Come on, Billy! Think you could maybe give me a little help here for once?" Mac covered the goal as best he could. To avoid the possibility of a lateral pass getting by him and placing the ball inside, he stayed pretty close to the net opening.

For a while, it worked. One attempt after

the other, the ball bounced off the goalposts or was deflected by his arm or his out-stretched palm.

But finally there were too many Bruins and too many shots on goal. After seven attempts in as many minutes, the eighth found its mark. The Bruins' right wing sent a low ball soaring toward the right corner of the net as Mac was recovering his balance from a concentrated effort to the left. His attempt to leap on the ball failed. He ended up on the ground as the ball hit the net. He lay there, the wind knocked out of him, as the scoring light went on, the ref's whistle blew, and the Bruins players on the bench jumped to their feet.

After a moment, Mac got up and steadied himself on the goalpost. He nodded to the coach that he was all right. His eyes then drifted to the stands. They were still applauding the Bruins' goal, but now the cheering was more scattered.

"Nice try, Mac!" he heard his mother yell from the corner where his parents usually sat.

That little bit of encouragement helped bring him back in the game.

Although it was his last time on the ground, Mac got a real workout during that first half. There were no more scores by either side, but both teams were determined to try for them. Mac had his work cut out for him — and he was up to it.

"Here they come! Here they come! Sweeper to the left! Move it, Billy! Get the lead out!" he shouted, all the while moving from one strategic position to another. Even when the ball was at the opposite end of the field, he called out to his teammates.

"Let's see your stuff there, Dougie! Heads up, Jackie!"

Noticing that Sam Napoli, a young Cougar midfielder, kept moving back and forth across the midfield stripe, Mac crooned out,

"Seesaw Sammy! Keep on swinging!" The fans rewarded that call with a ripple of laughter. Mac grinned, but turned serious again when he caught Billy Levine giving him a disgusted look.

What's his problem? Mac thought.

When the two teams trotted off the field at the halfway mark, the scoreboard still read, 1–0 in favor of the Bruins.

"You're doing everything right," said the coach. "Except you're not always taking advantage of your chances. They're outshooting you at goal almost two to one. Don't be intimidated by their reputation. Get tough. Don't get sloppy, though, just fierce!"

Mac gritted his teeth so hard, he was afraid they might break in half. When the whistle blew for the second half, he got into position, determined to defend his turf.

After the kickoff, the Cougars took possession of the ball. They held it down in Bruins territory for one goal attempt after another.

For a while, it looked as though the whole second half would be played down there.

That didn't stop Mac from keeping up his motion and his mouth work. He danced back and forth as he followed the play from afar. He wasn't surprised when the game turned around after the sixth unsuccessful goal attempt by the Cougars and the ball came zooming across the center line in his direction.

"C'mon, you Cougars, defense! Show 'em we're fierce animals, not pussycats!"

Mac glanced toward the stands as a ripple of laughter came from the fans. But a moment later that laughter turned to a gasp. Mac snapped his gaze back to the field, but he was too late. A Bruin had come out of nowhere, picked up a pass, and swiftly put the ball into the net before Mac knew what was happening.

The score now read, Bruins 2, Cougars 0.

"Looks like you're a pussycat after all, Cougar!" a Bruin wing called to Mac with a laugh.

Mac felt two feet tall. He knew he'd blown it, even though his attention had left the game for no more than a split second.

The Cougars were silent as they assembled for the kickoff. When the game resumed, Mac tried hard to get them back into the swing of it.

"Coverage, Billy, coverage!" he called to fill the void between him and the Bruins' wing who was threatening on one side.

"Get in there, Marv," he shouted, watching his Cougar teammate trying to wrestle the ball away from another opponent. "Dig in!"

Marv dug in a little too boldly, and the whistle blew, giving the Bruins a penalty shot.

Penalty shots were the most dreaded moments of Mac's day. He had one of the best records in the league for blocking such attempts, but the odds were still with the kicker.

The Bruins' right wing was all set to take the shot. Mac had been watching him throughout the game, and he thought he had detected a little weakness — a habit of trying for one particular corner of the net. If that held true, that's where he would try to put it now.

With that in mind, Mac got into position. Feet planted firmly on the ground, he glared at the kicker. Then when the Bruin began to run up for the kick, Mac shifted toward the "wrong" side of the net with his upper body — only to shift back at the last minute and dive in the opposite direction once the ball left the ground. His outstretched finger-tips just managed to connect with the ball and deflect it from going into the net.

The crowd went wild.

But there was no time for celebration. With the clock running down, the Cougars still hadn't gotten onto the scoreboard. They needed three quick goals to win this game.

It looked as though they might chalk up a goal as Dougie called for one of their sure-fire plays — a sweep around the midfielders followed by a quick charge right down the middle.

But a pass intended for Jackie got deflected off the heel of a Bruin defenseman. One of the Bruins' teammates was exactly in the right position and raced with the ball toward the Cougars' goal.

Billy tried to break the play, but with no luck. Mac was on his own.

He managed to block the first shot at the net but couldn't really get a grip on the ball. It bounced forward about ten feet, where it landed in front of a solitary Bruin forward. A second shot had no trouble going into the net.

The Bruins' fans cheered loudly, sure of a victory. With only thirty seconds left to play, there was no way the Cougars could win it now. They did their best, but in the end, the scoreboard read, Bruins 3, Cougars 0. It was their worst showing of the season.

Coach Robertson spoke quietly to them in the locker room. "Now we know what it's like to lose a tough one. So we learn from our experience. The season is still young, and there are a lot more games to play — and to win. Don't be too tough on yourselves. Just get some rest over the weekend, and I'll see you at practice on Monday."

**7**

**O**ver the weekend, Mac got together with Jimmy and Dougie to watch some movies at Jimmy's house. As the opening credits rolled by for the first video, Jimmy nudged Mac.

"Hey, I almost forgot to ask you guys if you're going to the dance the paper's hosting next week. I'm selling tickets."

Signs about the dance had been posted in the school hallways for the past week. It was going to be a casual affair, with a disc jockey and refreshments.

Dougie and Mac looked at each other. "A dance?" Dougie said. "I dunno. The last one I went to was a bust. All I did was stand at the edge of the gym and listen to music. I can listen to music at home for free."

"Hey, if you didn't have a good time, it was your own fault. You were too scared to ask Ann Leonard to dance with you," Mac said with a grin.

Dougie colored. "Yeah, well, I didn't see you out there too much, either. What's the matter, afraid whoever you'd ask would say no?"

With a twinkle in his eye, Jimmy said, "I know someone who would definitely say yes if you asked her, Mac."

Mac paused the video. "Oh, yeah? Who? Not that I'm interested, really."

"Let's just say that my kid sister has been asking an awful lot about soccer lately."

It was Mac's turn to blush, but secretly he was pleased. He wouldn't ever tell anyone, but he thought Jimmy's sister was kind of cute. "Deanna's not a kid," Mac said. "She's only a year younger than we are."

Jimmy and Dougie laughed. "The knight in shining armor defends his lady fair!" Dougie chortled.

"Cut it out! I am not! It's just that you made her sound like she was still in elementary school."

Jimmy, still grinning, said, "Well, you have my permission to ask her to boogie down with you if you want."

"Yeah, right," mumbled Mac as he clicked the movie back on. But somehow he couldn't concentrate on it anymore.

When it was over, he put on his most casual voice. "Jimmy, I guess if you're trying to unload those dance tickets, I'll take one."

Dougie and Jimmy cracked up. But Mac noticed that Dougie left with a ticket as well.

The following Monday, the *Chronicle* appeared with a new cartoon in the center. This time it was a drawing of a little cat in the middle of the goal. The cat was sound asleep, and a soccer ball was flying over its head. The caption underneath read, *Pussycat's catnap causes Cougars to lose!*

Mac saw red. He was tempted to find Margie Lewis and insist that she tell him who submitted it to the paper. Instead, he marched into the administration office and asked to speak to Dr. Witherspoon, the principal.

After a brief wait, he was ushered in.

"What can I do for you, Alfred?" asked the principal. A slender man with an outsized nose, he was probably the only person left in the whole world who used Mac's real first name.

"Well, sir," Mac said, "I don't know if you've seen the *Chronicle,* but this is the second time it's had a cartoon that makes fun of me. I don't know who's doing it, but I don't think it's really very nice. I want it stopped."

"Hmm, I see your point," said Dr. Witherspoon, looking at the page Mac held in front of him. "But I'm not sure that there's much I can do. You see, even though it's a school paper, it's protected by the Bill of Rights. You have studied that in your U.S. history class, haven't you?"

"Yes, sir, but —"

"Well, freedom of the press is one of our foremost rights," the principal went on. "Unless it's a case of libel, which I don't really see this as, the reporter or the artist does have a right to make his or her statement as he or she sees fit."

Mac's head was beginning to spin. "So anybody can say anything or draw somebody and make them look dumb and there's nothing you can do about it?"

"No," said the principal. "You may certainly respond to them in a letter to the editor. Or write an article yourself that points out where they're wrong."

"Oh, sure, so it'll make me look like I'm a bad sport or something," said Mac.

"Frankly, I don't think that it's as terrible as you do," said Dr. Witherspoon. "Remember how the paper made fun of me when I first came here?"

He patted his nose, and Mac suddenly recalled the drawing of him as Pinocchio that the paper had printed.

"You're right, sir," he admitted, smiling. "I guess we all have to take our knocks."

"Good, I'm glad you can see that," said the principal. "Ignore it. Or if you can't ignore it, make a game of trying to figure out who came up with the cartoon in the first place. I bet if you think hard enough, you'll come up with the culprit."

Mac left the principal's office mulling that last idea over.

He's right. I should be able to unveil the cartoonist, he thought. I just have to examine the clues. And the first clue is that the

48

cartoons were both about something that happened at a Cougars soccer game!

But by the time he'd reached the locker room for practice, he'd come to the conclusion that anybody — fans, teammates, even coaches — who had been at the last two soccer games could have drawn the cartoons. He was no closer to figuring it out than he'd been before.

Meanwhile, he had to face the ribbing of his teammates.

"Here, kitty, kitty, kitty," called Jackie as Mac trotted onto the field.

"I'll give you some nice catnip if you promise to stay awake today," Mickey added with a laugh.

"Maybe we should play with a ball of yarn instead of a soccer ball," Billy joked. "Then Mac would be sure to pounce!"

The whole team was practically doubled over with laughter. But the shrill sound of the coach's whistle put a quick end to it.

"Okay, let's start out by taking a few laps around the field to warm up. Maybe that will settle you down a little bit," the coach said.

The laps over, the coach ran a few drills, then split them into scrimmage squads and got down to the business of sharpening up their play.

As usual, Mac played the entire scrimmage in the goalie position for his squad. But unlike usual, his mind was only partially on the play. The rest of it was turning over the cartoon in his mind.

I have to narrow down the suspects, he thought. It's got to be someone who wants me to look like a fool. He turned that idea over in his mind a bit more. Someone on an opposite team, maybe?

He tossed that idea out as soon as he thought of it. The Cougars had played two different teams, so there was no way the cartoonist could have been there both times if he was from a rival squad. Plus, he was pretty sure the *Chronicle* only published material created by kids in their school.

Scratch that, he said to himself.

As the action continued down at the opposite end of the field, he had a new thought. What if it was someone on his own team?

He didn't have time to consider this thought for long. The sound of running feet alerted him that his squad had lost the ball to their opponents. The action was now at Mac's end of the field.

It was late in the day, and he could see that the play was getting sloppy. Passes skyrocketed off to places where there were no possible receivers. Players tripped over their own legs trying to wrestle the ball from an opponent. And too many shots were taken at the goal that didn't stand a chance of even getting near it.

Still, there was enough activity to keep Mac on his feet. He picked off several balls that came into his area and helped set up his squad time and time again.

After Mac snagged three shots in a row, it finally looked like the drift was to the opposite side of the field.

Mac took a few deep breaths and even leaned one arm on the side of the goal. He fanned his forehead with his other hand before shaking it off and moving to the center where he had a better view of the action.

A roar of victory came from across the field. Sammy had put one into the net. It was a score for his squad, the only one during the scrimmage.

Mac couldn't help grinning as he watched his teammates slap each other high fives and hurry back into position.

*There's no way the cartoonist is one of those guys,* he thought. *We're too tight a team for stuff like that. Besides, what would there be to gain by making fun of me?*

"What, no victory cry?" came a voice at

his elbow. It was Billy Levine. "What's the matter? Cat got your tongue?"

Mac's good mood vanished in an instant as he listened to Billy's laughter.

Then again, he thought, maybe we're not so tight after all.

**8**

For the next two days, Mac felt as though he were walking on eggshells. Even though he tried to put the *Chronicle* drawing out of his mind, he found himself eyeing everyone on the team suspiciously.

At the same time, he started being careful of what he said. He didn't want to give the cartoonist any more material to use as a theme for his next "work of art."

On Thursday, practice was rained out. A steady downpour washed over the area, and there was nothing to do but hunker down indoors after school had ended for the day.

Mac tried to catch up on some homework, but he really wasn't in the mood.

"You can always clean your room," his mother suggested. He knew that she must have been tired of having him wander in and out of the kitchen while she was trying to balance her checkbook.

"I already hung up my clothes," he said. "And I stacked everything else in neat piles."

"Well, I could clear out of here," she said. "And you could bake some cookies. You haven't done that in a while."

Mrs. Williams had taught all her children to do some cooking and baking. Mac's specialty was cookies. He never told her, but he liked nibbling on the raw dough as much as eating the final product.

"Nah, I'm not in the mood," he said.

"I'm sure there's nothing on TV," she said. "So why don't you just settle down and read a good book for a while. When I'm through, I'll challenge you to a game of cribbage."

"All right," said Mac without much enthu-
siasm.

He had started looking through his books
when he got an idea.

"Hey, Mom, I'm going to ask Dougie to
come over," he called into the kitchen. "We
can play cribbage some other time, okay?"

"Fine," replied his mother.

He dialed Dougie's number and made his
proposal.

"Hi, Dougie, you have that new *Soccer
Round the World* video, right?" he asked.

"Yeah, I told you my dad brought it home
the other night," said Dougie. "I haven't
taken a look at it yet, though. I thought I
might this afternoon."

"So why aren't you watching it right now?"
Mac asked.

Dougie whispered into the phone, "My
mother's got me doing things. She has a list
yards long of things that have been waiting
for a rainy day. And if I don't do them just

right . . . boy! We're really getting on each other's nerves, I think. Good thing she has to drop off some stuff at my grandmother's house."

"So why don't you just ask her to drop you off over here? Tell her you'll finish the list of stuff right when you get home. And bring the video. We can watch soccer even if we can't play it today," Mac suggested.

"Sounds good to me," said Dougie. "Hey, should we give Jimmy a call? Maybe he'd want to watch it with us."

"Naw, he can see it some other time," said Mac. "He reminds me of the paper, and I don't want to think about the *Chronicle* right now. Okay?"

After a brief conference with Dougie's mother, it was settled. She'd drop him off for an hour or so, then pick him up on her way back.

While he was waiting for Dougie, Mac took his mother's suggestion. In no time at all, he had a batch of chocolate chip cookies baking in the oven.

"Sure smells good in here," said Dougie when he arrived. He hung up his wet slicker in the mud room.

"It gets better," said Mac. "Go ahead and set the tape up. I'll be right back. Let me just get something from the kitchen."

He returned to the living room with a plate of warm cookies.

"They have to cool off, so don't burn your tongue," said Mac.

"Or even worse, yours!" said Dougie. "I mean, where would the Cougars be if you couldn't talk? Hmm, then again, maybe we'd all be able to get a word in edgewise for once!" He reached for a cookie and stuffed it in his mouth.

Mac didn't say anything. But inside, he wondered about what Dougie had said. Was it possible that Dougie was tired of listening to his chatter?

And if so, how far would he go to stop it? Far enough to submit a drawing to the school paper?

Mac shoved the thought from his mind. That's ridiculous, he said to himself. Dougie and I have been friends forever.

For the next half hour, they watched as teams from England, France, Brazil, Italy, Mexico, China, and a slew of other countries played parts of one soccer match after another. There were no full games on the tape, but the highlights made up for it.

One play in particular caught their eye. "Wow!" Mac cried. "Look at that pass! Talk about 'threading the needle' — whew!"

"Stop the tape and rewind it," said Dougie. "Let's see it again."

They watched it no less than three times — a forward on the Italian team booting an amazing pass. The ball went cross-corner through the legs of one defenseman, behind the back of another, off the heel of a third, and ended up in perfect position at the outside edge of the penalty area. It gave another forward a clear shot at the goal, which he took.

But the defending goalie managed to get the ball on a forward vault before it went into the net.

"See, once again, the goalie makes for the win or loss," said Mac, clenching his fists together over his head and stretching.

"Oh, really? So I guess what I do doesn't amount to anything," said Dougie, his voice dripping with sarcasm.

"I didn't mean that. You know all the goals you've scored are important," said Mac.

"Just important? Maybe you're forgetting that it's the goals I earn that win the game — not the number of goals you save," said Dougie hotly.

"Oh, and I suppose you think I don't save enough goals, do you? I bet you think I'm asleep on the job or too busy talking to play good soccer, just like those stupid cartoons say, don't you? Maybe you're even the one who drew them!"

The minute the words left his mouth, Mac wished he could take them back. Dougie was his best friend. What Mac had accused him of was ludicrous.

Dougie didn't say anything. He just stood up and pushed the rewind button on the VCR.

Mac felt miserable. "Listen, Dougie —," he started to say.

Dougie cut him off. "Just because one person who can draw is poking fun at you doesn't mean everyone is against you."

"I know, and I'm sorry, Dougie. I know it isn't you. But why am I the target?" asked Mac. "Why isn't anyone poking fun at you, for instance?"

"I don't know," his friend replied. "Maybe I'm not a big enough cheese."

"But you're the number one scorer on the team!" Mac exclaimed.

"Yeah, but you talk like a big shot most of the time," said Dougie. "So people are more aware of you than they are of me. And you know, there may be some people who don't appreciate all you have to say."

Mac shook his head.

"So what should I do? Just shut up and play?"

Dougie snickered. "As if you could!" He settled back in his chair, munching on a cookie. Through the crumbs in his mouth he said, "Listen, we'll figure out who's doing those cartoons. But in the meantime, let's test you through the rest of this video. I'll bet you the last cookie that you can't make it through three plays without making a noise!"

"Deal!"

Two plays later, Dougie was polishing off the last morsel, grinning from ear to ear.

**9**

By Friday, Mac had again managed to bury some of his feelings about the phantom cartoonist. Luckily he had other things to think about — like the game that afternoon and the school dance that would follow. He, Dougie, and Jimmy were going to go to the dance together "because," as Dougie pointed out, "there's safety in numbers!"

The hallways were filled with excited talk of the dance all day. At lunch, Mac joined his usual group of friends. He had just taken a huge bite of his peanut butter sandwich when Jimmy asked in a loud voice, "So, Mac, is my kid sister, Deanna, going to get all dolled up for nothing tonight?"

Mac sputtered but couldn't get a word out around his sticky mouthful.

"He's speechless! Ladies and gentlemen, it's a first!" Jimmy chortled. "There's something for the papers!"

While the rest of the guys laughed, Mac stared at Jimmy. A thought had suddenly crossed his mind.

Could Jimmy have something to do with those cartoons?

He hadn't considered the possibility before, but the more he thought about it, the more it all seemed to fit. Jimmy had connections at the paper. He attended every game, including the two that came before the cartoons. He had been the lead scorer for the Cougars' rivals only last year; maybe his loyalties were still with that team. Or maybe he was more upset than he let on that Coach Robertson had told Mac he'd take his help on the sidelines — yet had refused to let Jimmy lend a hand.

The evidence was only circumstantial, but it added up just the same.

"Jimmy?" Dougie repeated incredulously when Mac told him his suspicions after lunch. "You're kidding, right? Jimmy hasn't got a mean bone in his body. No way is it him."

"I don't want to believe it, either," Mac admitted. "But everything points to him!"

Dougie shook his head. "You're going to have to do better than that to convince me."

"Okay, then let's set a trap for him!"

"Trap? What kind of trap?" Dougie wanted to know.

Mac thought for a moment. Then he snapped his fingers. "I know. At today's game, I'll do or say something stupid when only you two are around. If it winds up as a cartoon, then we'll know it's him!"

"I guess that could work," Dougie mused.

Then he cracked a huge smile. "Of course, you're always saying and doing so many stupid things, it'll be hard for me to know which one is supposed to be the trap!"

"Hardy har har," Mac said.

"Oh, good comeback." Dougie gave Mac a friendly shove, then took off for his next class. "See you later in the locker room, genius!"

Mac knew he had to come up with something really good to test Jimmy with. And he had to be sly about it. If Jimmy was the cartoonist, he might suspect Mac was on to him if he was too obvious.

But what to do or say? Mac puzzled about that through the rest of his classes.

It came to him during the coach's pre-game pep talk.

"Okay, listen up," Coach Robertson called. The team gathered around him. As usual, Jimmy Palumbo was sitting in, hoping for an inspiring quote to start off his weekly column. "I know you guys don't think that the Blue Sox are that much of a threat because they have a really poor record so far. Well, I'm telling all of you that you have to be on your special guard today. There are two enemies out there. There's the Blue Sox, with their losing record for the season. And there's complacency. That's right. You could be your own worst enemy if you take it for granted that you're better than they are and try to coast through the game.

"But you can't. Every single one of you has to give it everything you have — or they'll end up walking all over you. That goes for you wings. It goes for you midfielders. It goes for the backfield, for the defense, for the sweeper. And Mac, as our last hope, it's up to you to be on your toes. Now get out there and do your best."

"Go, Cougars!" Mac led the cheer as the

huddle around the coach broke up and the team headed for the field. Then Mac suddenly stopped.

"Dougie, Jimmy, I can't find my gloves! Can you guys give me a hand?"

"A hand to find your gloves?" Dougie echoed. "Pretty funny."

Jimmy started digging through the mess in the bottom of Mac's locker. Mac pretended to search the floor, and Dougie pawed through his duffel bag.

Mac cleared his throat. "Hey, did you guys catch how the coach called me 'the last hope'? Just goes to show you how highly he thinks of me."

Dougie snorted. "Yeah, but he also warned you to keep on your toes, don't forget."

Mac gave Dougie a significant look. Dougie glanced at Jimmy's back, and raised an eyebrow at Mac.

"Keep on my toes?" Mac repeated, then

waited a beat until he was sure Jimmy was watching him. "You mean, like a ballerina? Like this?" With a simpering look plastered to his face, he circled his arms above his head, raised himself up on the balls of his feet, and tippytoed across the floor.

Jimmy and Dougie cracked up. Then a holler from the field reminded Mac and Dougie that they had a game to play.

"Yikes! Let's go!" Mac cried.

"Wait, what about your gloves?" Jimmy asked.

"Hey, what do you know? They were in my gym bag the whole time!"

"Oh, brother. Listen, I'll see you guys later. Dougie, your mom's picking us up for the dance at seven o'clock sharp, right?" Jimmy called as he ran to the stands.

Dougie nodded, and he and Mac joined the rest of the team on the bench.

"Well," Mac said. "That oughta do it. Now

we sit back and see what appears in the paper on Monday."

"Forget Monday. Let's concentrate on to-day — and winning this game!" Dougie cried as the team took to the field.

Okay, you Cougars! Show 'em your stuff, Dougie! Mickey, put 'em where they belong! Mel, you've got the muscle! Billy, try giving me a hand today, what do you say? Cougars! Cougars! Eat 'em up alive!"

The Blue Sox had won the toss and elected to kick off.

Mac stared down the field toward the center spot as the two teams lined up. He took a deep breath, and the game began.

The kick went toward a Blue Sox halfback, who tried to nudge the ball to one of their forwards. But the Cougars swarmed in and managed to snag it. The halfback was left standing alone as the ball went off in the other direction.

Mickey took control of the ball and led the charge toward the goal, passing it back and forth with Stevie, who paralleled him down the field.

But the Blue Sox weren't rolling over. Even from his distance, Mac could see that they were all set to play a strong, hard game.

"Set 'em up, Mickey! Set 'em up! Watch out for those Blues! In there, Dougie! Find your spot!" His chatter continued as long as the ball was in play.

Every now and then Mickey managed to send the ball through the maze of players to the opposite side of the field. The Cougars had several plays that started out with Stevie on the right side facing the goal. But every time, as though it had a bungee cord attached to it, the ball sprang back to the left side of the field.

"Set it up, Mickey! Come on, Dougie!" Mac called. The Blue Sox defense was tougher than the Cougars had thought it would be, but Mac could tell that they were weakest in the middle. The Cougars had the best chance of scoring by concentrating their efforts there.

Mac knew Dougie was the key to play in the middle. And sure enough, when Dougie got ahold of the ball a moment later, he didn't give it up easily. He quickly dodged around the Blue Sox sweeper. And then, before the Sox knew what was happening, he took a shot.

The lightning quick move surprised the Sox goalie. The ball sailed into the net, giving the Cougars an early lead.

As the crowd cheered, Mac smiled. A lot of people thought that Dougie was just lucky. Mac knew better. Dougie had an incredible sense of timing, combined with an ability to keep track of everything that was going on around him. It was no wonder he was the team's leading scorer.

As the two teams gathered back at the center of the field for the next kickoff, Mac could hear Jimmy Palumbo shouting, "Dougie does it! Dougie does it! Go, you Cougars!"

Listening to him suddenly made Mac wonder if he'd been right to put Jimmy at the top of his suspect list. He sure didn't sound like a guy whose loyalty was with another team.

But the evidence . . .

Mac didn't have time to spend thinking about Jimmy. After a brief spell down at the other goal, the action moved toward him. The Cougars' offensive line had let up enough for the Blue Sox to gain control of the ball. They brought it down toward Mac with a lot more precision than he'd expected.

This was definitely no second-rate team, he realized.

At the same time, he could tell that the

Cougars' defense wasn't quite ready for what was taking place. Within moments, only Mac and Billy stood between the Blue Sox and a goal.

"Position! Position, Billy, come on, watch your position! Billy, stay on top of him! Heads up!" he called from the back of the penalty zone.

*Thwap!* A Blue Sox forward dodged around Billy and booted the ball toward the goal. It was a long shot, but it came close. Mac leaped and just managed to deflect it before it went into the net.

Lucky the old springs are working, Mac said to himself as he got back his balance. But I sure could use a little help! What's up with Billy?

The deflected ball bounced off Billy's shoulder and tumbled back to the ground near a Blue Sox forward. A battle for control went on and on as others joined in and the struggle became more heated.

*Tweeeeet!* The referee's whistle signaled a foul.

The call was on the Cougars. It seemed that in his determination to get the ball, Billy had grabbed hold of the forward's shirt and held on to him. It was a major violation, and there would be a direct free kick.

"Aw, jeez, Billy," Mac groaned. "Okay, Cougars, let's not let that mistake ruin our lead. Come on, line up!"

The Cougars had practiced forming a wall against such penalty kicks. It was time to put that practice into operation. Mac's job now was to see that they were exactly where he needed them to be.

Although the Cougars stood shoulder to shoulder, there was still plenty of clearance where the ball might go in. A lot depended on the skill of the Blue Sox kicker. And ultimately, it was up to Mac to be in the right spot at the right time.

He ranged behind them, lining them

up, softly whispering his directions.

"A little to the left. Open up just an inch or so. That's it, that's it. Okay," he murmured.

Suddenly it was happening. *Thud!* The kick was in the air. It wasn't a very good kick and missed the opening by quite a distance. Simply standing there, Mickey took it on his kneecap before it ricocheted forward. Mac didn't even get to see the ball before play resumed.

Breathing a sigh of relief, he went back to defending the goal area. The ball was still in Cougar territory, and the threat wasn't over.

Both teams were playing a sloppy game, and there were endless offside calls, followed by tangles where no one was really in command of the ball.

One of those clumps of players formed just to the edge of the penalty area, and Mac could barely see where the ball was — until too late.

It squirted free, and a Blue Sox forward

managed to tip it into the goal with a short kick from an undefended corner.

Mac slammed his fists down onto his knees. He was so angry that he hadn't anticipated the shot. Even though he knew it was impossible to block every ball from going into the net, he had been hoping to keep the Blue Sox off the scoreboard for a little longer. The way the Cougars were playing, particularly defense, they needed all the help they could get.

For the rest of the first half, the two teams slogged back and forth across the field. There was no scoring and little accomplished. Except for wearing one another down.

"See, it's not a pushover, is it?" Coach Robertson said as the Cougars gathered at the bench. "You're more tired than you usually are at this point, aren't you? That's because you're using more muscle than brains out there. You're just not thinking."

"So what do we do now?" asked Mel.

"You start using your noggins," said the coach. "And I'm not talking about just heading the ball. Start playing as a team again. Keep your eyes on your teammates as well as the ball. Look for the openings, and make the best of them."

"Coach, I noticed something," Mac piped up. "It might not mean anything, but maybe it does."

He pointed out what he had observed about the Blues' weak middle of the field defense.

"Even when subs go in, the defense just isn't strong there," Mac said.

"Good point," said the coach. "With your line of sight, that's a good pickup. Offense, keep that in mind. Get the ball to Dougie when he's in front of the goal. But defense, make sure you still clear the ball to the sides. Otherwise, Mac will be in trouble."

Mac was pleased at the coach's reaction

to what he had observed. He was happy that he could make a real contribution. He was determined to concentrate on what was happening out there and see if he noticed anything else that might help.

Such concentration helped keep his mind off the mysterious cartoonist. For the time being, anyway.

**11**

**H**alfway through the second half of the game, the scoreboard still read, Cougars 1, Blue Sox 1. Scoring had bogged down, and neither side seemed able to get the ball into the net.

The coach had changed his forward line now. He had taken Dougie from the center and put him into the left wing position. With his usual tenacity, Dougie managed to set up one goal attempt after another. But save after save followed.

Frustrated by the lack of scoring, Mac started calling out encouragement. Only now he had to yell loud to be heard at the opposite end of the field, where so much of the action was taking place.

He was practically hoarse when the game turned in his direction. A loose ball skittered into the far corner. Billy chased it, got control, and turned to boot it upfield.

To Mac's horror, Billy sent the ball into the middle of the field instead of up the lines. Two Blue Sox midfielders were ready and waiting. They brought the ball right down to the penalty area and lined up a shot.

Mac did his best to read them, but these were two new guys fresh off the bench. He faked a little in one direction, hoping to lure the ball the other way, but it was no use. From an angle just off center, the ball went zooming across him into the far corner of the net for a goal.

Now the scoreboard read, Blue Sox 2, Cougars 1.

"Billy!" Mac yelled. "What were you thinking?"

Billy scowled. "Coach said to set up the plays in the middle of the field. Or weren't you listening?"

"Yeah, I was listening. And I heard him say for the *defense* to keep clearing the ball to the sides! Where were you when he said that?"

Billy didn't reply. He hunched his shoulders and turned his attention to the center of the field, where play was about to resume.

What's with that guy? Mac thought for the second time that day.

There was still five minutes left on the clock. Plenty of time to catch up and turn the score around.

"Come on, Dougie! Let's go, Jackie! I know you can do it, Mickey!"

A light wind drifted across the field and seemed to scatter Mac's words to the four corners of the field as the softest of whispers.

And for all the good they did, they might as well have been the utterances of a ghost. When the final whistle blew, the score remained the same. The Blue Sox had gained a victory, and the Cougars dropped a notch in the league standings.

After lining up and performing the ritual of handshakes with the winners, the defeated Cougar team jogged off the field into their locker room.

Other than the sounds of locker doors slamming and equipment being banged around, it was quiet as the team got cleaned up and ready to leave. The coach had little to say except that he'd see them at practice on Monday.

"Any notable quotables?" Jimmy asked, sitting on the bench near Mac's locker. "Come on, Mac, you're never at a loss for words."

Mac just shook his head.

"Dougie? Stevie? Mel? Anyone have anything to say?"

As if by mutual consent, the whole team remained silent.

"Okay, I'll put away my notepad," said Jimmy. "Whatever you say is off the record. What went wrong out there?"

Mickey mumbled something about the coach being right. "And that's all I'm going to say," he added.

"He was right on the money," Mac agreed. "I could see it all the way across the field. Missed opportunities, one after another."

For the next few minutes, Mac held forth on everything that everyone had done wrong. And he was on the mark every time; no one could disagree with that.

When he paused, Jimmy spoke up. "And what about you, Mac? What about your game?"

The whole locker room was suddenly silent. Waves of tension filled every corner as each player awaited Mac's reply.

Mac stared Jimmy straight in the eye and said coldly, "I was as bad as everyone else, no doubt about it. You can report that — along with whatever else it is you're going to print."

**12**

**M**ac got a phone call soon after he walked through his kitchen door after the game. It was Jimmy.

"Hey, you mad at me or something?" Jimmy asked.

Mac mumbled something about being disappointed about the game.

"Well, I hope your mood gets better. Don't forget, we have a dance to go to tonight! Though from what I saw in the locker room before the game today, I don't think I want to be caught near you on the dance floor."

Mac said, "Yeah, I'm a real comedian. But we'll see who gets the last laugh."

After dinner, Mac took a long shower. The hot water seemed to take away a lot of the tension he was feeling. Halfway through toweling himself off, he decided to take Dougie's advice and put the cartoons out of his mind until Monday. If it was Jimmy, he'd find out then. If it wasn't, he didn't want to risk ruining their friendship by acting cold. Besides, he didn't want to give anything away by behaving differently.

By the time Dougie's mom stopped by to pick him up, he was determined to treat Jimmy just as he always did.

Dougie and Jimmy were already in the car. "You're looking spiffy," Jimmy said as Mac slid into the seat beside him. "You do that for Deanna?"

Dougie grinned as Mac turned bright red.

Dougie's mother dropped them off at the school gym. Inside, colored lights flashed, streamers fluttered in air currents, and music boomed from big speakers set up in the corners. Hordes of kids were dancing while other groups stood around the outskirts of the room or by the refreshment table.

Mac, Dougie, and Jimmy made a beeline for the food. They filled their napkins with cookies and brownies, then grabbed cups of punch. Hands full, they looked around for other people they knew.

"Hey, there's Mickey and Jackie," Mac said. The three boys made their way across the floor to the others. They all exchanged greetings, then turned their attention to the dance floor.

"Look at Mel!" said Dougie. "He's dancing with Sandra McCloud! Man, the guy is all arms and legs!"

"Maybe we should call him 'the octopus,' " Jimmy joked.

"And there's Sam Napoli, with Joan Rockport. Do you think he could get any closer to her?" Dougie went on.

"Yeah, he's a real space invader," Jimmy

agreed. "Wonder which planet he's from. Get it?"

Listening to Jimmy, Mac's suspicions suddenly flared up again. He gave Jimmy a sidelong look. "You're pretty quick with those nicknames and stuff," he said.

Jimmy laughed. "I got a million of 'em!" he said.

I bet you do, Mac couldn't stop himself from thinking. And I bet they come in handy when you do your cartoons.

"Hey, there's Billy!" Dougie's cry interrupted his thoughts. "Billy, come on over here!"

Mac saw Billy glance in their direction and frown. He said something to the girl he was with, then the two of them came over to Mac's group. Mac didn't recognize the girl at first, until Jimmy greeted her.

"Hi, Margie, taking time off from the newspaper, or are you here as a reporter?"

Margie Lewis answered coolly, "It

wouldn't look very good if the editor of the paper didn't show up at the dance the *Chronicle* was throwing, now would it? And if I see something that's worth putting in the paper, then I've killed two birds with one stone, haven't I?"

The boys had no reply to that, so they sipped their punch and ate their snacks in silence. Then Jimmy announced he had to go to the bathroom. "But you don't have to put that in the paper, Margie," he said in a stage whisper as he left.

Mac finished up the last of his punch and tossed his cup in the trash. All he had left from the refreshment table was a brownie. Just as he shoved the whole thing in his mouth at once, he felt a tap on his shoulder.

He turned around to see Deanna Palumbo standing in front of him.

"Hi, Mac," she said brightly. She was looking really sharp in a pair of jeans and a T-shirt with a blazer over it.

Mac, his mouth full of brownie, couldn't speak at first. Then, to his horror, when he tried to say hello, he sprayed Deanna with a light shower of crumbs! As his face turned beet red, he heard Dougie and the other soccer players sniggering.

Finally he swallowed. "Hi, Deanna," he said lamely. "Jimmy said you'd be here."

"Where *is* Jimmy?" Deanna asked.

"He'll be back in a second. Uh, so, what do you think of the dance?"

Deanna gave him an impish smile. "Come out on the dance floor with me, and maybe I'll tell you!"

Before Mac could think of an excuse, she had whisked him into the middle of the dancers. Mac was sure he looked ridiculous and couldn't stop thinking about the way he and the others had poked fun at their friends.

Boy, I'd hate to hear what they're saying about me, he thought, sneaking a peek at them.

Yet to his amazement, he found that he was enjoying himself. Deanna was a good dancer, and in time his natural athletic ability took over and he stopped jerking around like a puppet with a few broken strings.

He relaxed even more when he saw other friends on the floor: Mel and Sandra stayed together a lot of the time, and Billy and Margie danced every so often. Even Dougie had screwed up enough courage to ask Ann Leonard to dance.

Time flew by, and before Mac could believe it, the lights came up and the disc jockey announced that the dance was over. But after a game of soccer and a night of dancing, he was tired enough to be ready to go home.

Jimmy, who had been dancing with one of Deanna's friends, took a ride home with Deanna, the friend, and some other kids instead of Dougie and Mac. The two exhausted friends were quiet most of the way home, but when the car pulled into Mac's driveway,

Dougie asked, "So, tell me. Do you still think Jimmy is the cartoonist?"

Mac leaned down into the open door. "I hope not. Deanna's really nice and I was kind of thinking of asking her to a movie next week. But how can I if her brother has it in for me?"

"Guess we'll find out on Monday," Dougie said as he closed the door.

Mac stood in the driveway for a moment, then muttered, "Yeah, I guess we will."

**13**

"**A**re you ready for today's paper?" Dougie asked him when they met up at lunch on Monday.

"Yeah," said Mac. "Just make sure I'm not anywhere near Jimmy when it comes out. Just in case."

"You got it," promised Dougie.

But Dougie couldn't keep his promise. Moments later, Jimmy and a few other boys joined them at the table. Jimmy sat down, then with a flourish handed Mac a copy of the *Chronicle*.

"Hot off the presses," he said. "I haven't

even looked at it yet. Thought you'd like the honors."

"Oh, man," said Mel from beside Jimmy. "I hope it doesn't have another dumb drawing in it."

All eyes turned to Mac to see what he felt about that.

"You mean, the one that's being drawn by the head of my fan club? Gee, I can't remember if I told him to put one in this week," he said sarcastically. But his heart was racing as he opened the paper to the center section.

Everything was quiet for a moment, then Dougie broke the silence.

"Well, at least the cartoonist didn't picture you in the goal this time."

Even so, everyone knew who was the brunt of the joke. Nervous laughter broke out around the table.

Mac stared at the cartoon. It showed a boy in a Cougars goalie uniform dancing with a girl wearing a blazer. Not only was the boy looking like he had no control over his limbs, but the artist had also shown him trying to talk to the girl — and failing because his mouth was crammed full of food. Instead of words coming out, he was showering his dance partner with crumbs.

The caption underneath read, *Bet she wishes Motor Mouth would keep his trap shut (who doesn't!?).*

Mac crumpled up the paper, then raised his eyes to look at Jimmy. Jimmy's grin faded, and he cleared his throat. "I wonder if my sister's seen this," he said.

Mac tossed the wad at him and said savagely, "You mean you didn't even ask her if it was okay to put her in your latest cartoon?"

Jimmy's eyes widened. "What?"

"You heard me! I guessed it was you a while ago, so you can forget about the innocent looks!"

Dougie coughed. "Uh, Mac, I think you're

97

forgetting something —," he started to say.

"Dougie, keep out of this," Mac snarled.

"But Mac —"

"I mean it! This is between Jimmy and me. So how 'bout it Jimmy? You gonna confess finally or what?"

Jimmy stood up, his fists clenched. "You've already tried and convicted me, so what is there for me to say?" He picked up his lunch things and stormed off.

The other boys quickly and silently ate their lunches, then melted away with a few mumbled excuses. Finally only Dougie and Mac remained at the table.

"Mac, I wish you had let me say something before you cheesed off at Jimmy," Dougie said.

Mac sighed. "Okay, what is it?"

"It's just that I don't think the cartoonist is Jimmy after all. In fact, I'm sure of it."

"Why?"

"Because Jimmy wasn't there when your mouth was so full of brownie that you couldn't speak to Deanna. He was in the bathroom, remember? So how could he use that in his cartoon?"

Mac stared at Dougie as the truth of that fact sunk in. Then he slumped across the table.

"I really blew it, didn't I?" he said dejectedly. "Some detective I'd make. But Dougie, if it isn't Jimmy, who *is* it?"

Both boys were silent for a while. Jimmy let his eyes roam around the room. Suddenly his gaze stopped on someone.

"I'm not positive," he said, still staring. "But the possibilities are a lot narrower now. It had to have been someone who was standing with us at the dance, right?"

Dougie nodded.

Mac shifted his glance to his friend. "So what do you say we try laying another trap?

And this time, we'll be sure our net catches the right culprit!"

"I'm in," Dougie agreed enthusiastically.

"Good. Now all I have to do is get Jimmy to forgive me. Because without him, my plan won't work!"

Mac cornered Jimmy in the hallway later that day. Jimmy tried to get around him, but Mac wouldn't budge.

"Jimmy, I want to apologize. I went crazy when I saw that cartoon. Shoot, I've *been* crazy ever since I saw the first one. But I — I should have known you were too good a friend to pull something rotten like that."

Jimmy was quiet for a moment, then he sighed. "I guess I know why you thought it was me," he said. "I do work for the paper, after all. And I was at the games where you said those things the cartoonist made fun of. And probably the fact that I used to play for the Hornets didn't escape your memory."

"You read my mind! Except you forgot about how the coach mentioned he'd use my help on the sidelines if I ever got injured."

Jimmy gave him a wry smile. "Thanks for reminding me. Now I feel a *lot* better."

Mac gulped. "Aw, Jimmy, don't —"

Jimmy's laughter cut him off. "Don't worry, pal," he said, giving Mac a light punch in the arm. "I got over that a long time ago. I like reporting on the games. And besides, once next season rolls around and the coach sees my stuff, he'll be begging me to break another bone so I can be on the sidelines with him!"

Mac grinned. "For a moment there, I thought I'd blown it again! But since I'm forgiven, Jimmy, I wonder if you would like to join Dougie and me in a little sting operation to catch the real culprit. We're calling it Operation Payback."

"You got a deal!"

"Great! Meet me at my house tonight so

I can tell you all the details. Now if you'll excuse me, I have to try to convince Coach Robertson to join our plan, too."

By the time Mac crawled into bed that night, he had secured Coach Robertson's agreement to go along with his plan. Dougie and Jimmy had come over as promised, and together they had hashed out the finer points of Operation Payback.

"I just hope this doesn't backfire on you, Mac," Dougie had said once. "If it does, you could find yourself facing more than one onslaught of offense single-handedly."

Mac had shrugged, saying, "It'll be worth it if it stops those lousy cartoons."

As he stared at his ceiling now, he mulled over his plan one last time. He finally fell asleep convinced that it was foolproof — and that his suspicions about the cartoonist's identity would be confirmed when the *Chronicle* came out on Monday.

**14**

**F**riday morning was one of the coldest of the year.

"You ought to be wearing down parkas to play today," said Mrs. Williams, pouring a second cup of cocoa for Mac.

"It'll warm up," he said. "Besides, during a game you don't even have a chance to think about the cold."

"Unless you're in the stands like your father and me," she said. "Or on the sidelines. But I guess you don't get much time away from the goal."

"Nope," he said.

"Well, at least one of us will be toasty," she said.

But by game time, the cold had moved on and it was a beautiful, sunny day.

The sparkling green field under the blue sky looked particularly colorful as the Hotspurs in their deep-blue-and-orange uniforms shared space with the Cougars in their usual bright-yellow-and-black attire.

"Okay, Cougars! Everyone who's ready to get those Hotspurs, give me a high five!" Mac called, holding his hands in the air.

His teammates ran by him and slapped one palm or the other. All but one of them gave him a conspiratorial wink.

Those were the signals Mac was looking for. They told him that Dougie and Jimmy had completed their part of Operation Payback. Mac had asked his friends to tell all but one of his teammates about the plan. That way, when it came time for him to do his "acting job" in front of the coach, everyone but the suspect would know that his behavior was just a smoke screen.

If Mac's suspicions were correct, the cartoonist wouldn't be able to resist using Mac's performance as Monday's cartoon. And then Mac would have him!

When the ref's whistle blew to start the game, the Cougars lined up, raring to go. A strong effort from their two wings might just start things off on the right track. Just as important, it gave them a broader defense against the powerful league leaders in scoring. The Hotspurs were definitely going to keep Mac on his toes.

He felt up to it. He'd been practicing hard all week, and his instincts were razor sharp. Now all he needed was to keep his focus on the game. Operation Payback wouldn't begin until halftime.

The kickoff went well for the Cougars. Within seconds of play, they had the ball in Hotspur territory. Within two minutes, they had taken their first shot on goal. Dougie had risked a slightly oblique angle on an open strip of space. The ball hit a defending Hotspur a few feet from the goal area. But it sent out a message. This was going to be a hard-fought game.

"Come on, you Cougars! Show 'em your stuff, guys! Nice try, Dougie!"

Mac's stream of encouragement went on as usual. Sometimes the fans joined in with him; sometimes they didn't seem to notice that he was even there. That was standard for a goalie, he knew. Still, it was nice when they responded to something he had shouted.

Even better was when he was able to help his team. Many of the opposing players paid little attention to what came from his mouth.

And that's just the way he liked it. Their mistakes were highlighted more and more as parts of Mac's ongoing patter. When the play came down to the Cougars' goal, this could mean a big difference.

"Back! Back! Mickey, go back! You're losing 'Big Red' there! Come on, Stevie! Heads up, ball's coming your way! Right wing's fancy dancing, guys. Watch for the pass!"

Mac could see how hard the Cougars were trying to keep the ball from coming his way. But that didn't prevent the occasional Hotspur boot being taken at the goal.

"Left wing on the march!" he shouted, just before the tall, bespectacled Hotspur forward let fly in his direction.

Mac extended his hands, joining the thumbs together, and leaped for the top section of the net. His outstretched fingers managed to deflect the ball as it started its descent toward its target. The ball fell to the ground in the penalty area a few feet in front of the net. Mel, who had seen Mac do that move a hundred times, was right there to snag the ball and send it in the opposite direction.

A snarl of defensive Hotspurs broke up any

chance for a quick "rebound" attempt. For the next several minutes, the ball was passed back and forth between the two teams with no real movement toward the goal or the opposite side of the field. And as often as the ball went out of bounds, it always seemed to stay in the same area once it was thrown back into play.

Mac could tell that the Hotspurs were surprised that they hadn't managed to score yet. From what he'd read or heard about their other games, they were used to getting onto the scoreboard first, and early in the game at that. At least the Cougars had succeeded in breaking that pattern. It could be what was needed to break their stride and cause them to make mistakes.

But so far neither side had made many visible mistakes. Except for the occasional ball out of bounds, few penalty whistles blew. Basically it was a pretty clean game. That's why it was a surprise when a major foul was called on Billy for tripping.

The kicker was the tall redheaded wing who had been frustrated in three shots at the goal so far.

Mac tried to read him as he lined up his wall to defend the goal. But "Red" was a real stone-face. His deep brown eyes gave away nothing.

There was complete silence on the field and in the stands as the approach was taken. *Thwunk!*

It was much too high! Mac didn't even have to extend himself as the ball sailed over the net. He could practically hear the sigh of relief from the Cougars as play resumed.

Inspired by their defensive work, the Cougars dug in and turned the ball around in the other direction. Dougie dominated the play as the ball inched closer and closer to the goal. There was no way that the Cougars were going to let the first half of this game end without a score.

"Team play! Team play!" Mac hollered from his lonesome post at the opposite end of the field. He wanted them to remember to set up plays that had been worked out in scrimmages that week. True, a good player always had to be alert to an opening for a goal shot, but just as many goals were scored on well-worked-out plays.

Mac's voice must have penetrated someone's head, because a Cougars offensive play was set up. Dougie made the fake, then took the shot. The ball zoomed behind the goalie and into the net for the first score of the game.

The scoreboard now showed one goal — for the Cougars.

Mac raced downfield toward the center to embrace his teammates as they celebrated their goal. He then quickly ran back into his defensive position. He thought the Hotspurs had a mean look about them that said they weren't happy with the way things were going — and they were determined to change it.

His prediction turned out to be true — oh, too true.

Like a repeater rifle, the Hotspurs managed to set up one shot after another. They came so fast, Mac had his work cut out for him.

But even his talent and determination were no match for the Hotspurs. The onslaught proved to be indefensible. By the time the whistle blew signaling the end of the first half of the game, the scoreboard read, Hotspurs 2, Cougars 1.

Mac trotted off the field toward the Cougars' bench. There was a cool east wind blowing across the field. Still, he could feel warm beads of sweat trickling down the parts of his back where his shirt wasn't stuck fast. His legs ground out the distance to the spot where the team had gathered around the water barrel.

"Cool off for a minute," the coach was saying as he got there. "Just have some water and let yourselves relax for a few minutes."

Mac got his water in a paper cup. He quickly let it slide down the back of his throat with his head thrown slightly back. It felt terrific for a moment. But it took two refills to quench his thirst — and prepare his voice for the performance he was about to give.

"All of you are playing a solid game," the coach began, once the team had drunk their fill. "But you're playing it too close and too tight. The result is that no one ever seems to have the big picture of what's happening on the field. Except Mac, sometimes."

"So, what is the big picture, coach?" asked Dougie, right on cue.

"I'll answer that question!" Mac said suddenly. With an aggressive move, he placed himself right in front of Coach Robertson.

Although all his teammates but one knew what was coming, many of them looked surprised at his boldness just the same. Mac cleared his throat and began his harangue.

"Offense, you're rushing your kicks. You had half a dozen good setups that you blew because you didn't take enough time lining up the shot. And you're starting to get ahead of yourselves there, too. You know what I mean. Your heads are coming up too fast. When you're shooting at that target, once you've lined it up, keep your eye on the ball, for Pete's sake."

"It feels like they're breathing down my neck, sometimes," said Dougie.

"Hah! They're all over the backfield most of the time," said Mac. "Believe me, I can see 'em."

"Thank you, Mac —," the coach started to say. But Mac cut him off.

"You midfielders could help out a little more, too, you know. Help the forwards set up plays instead of standing back and admiring a pass you just made. And forwards, trust your instincts about the goal shot and go for it."

"I don't suppose you have any thoughts about the defense, do you?" the coach asked, his voice heavy with sarcasm.

"All I know is I felt like a duck at a shooting gallery, so a little more help from my sweeper and backs would be greatly appreciated!"

Just then the ref's whistle blew, signaling the start of the second half.

"Yeah, Cougars, let's go for it!" shouted Mac. "Come on, team!"

As Mac hurried to his position, he stole a look at his suspect's face to see if he could read any kind of reaction to his performance in it. But the face was stony, intent on the game at hand.

Still, Mac was sure he had the right guy.

All in good time, he said to himself.

His cheering was stronger than ever as the team took its position for the kickoff.

The Hotspurs were quick to attack. Within two minutes of the second half, they had added another goal to their score.

It was booted in by that same redhead who had threatened with the penalty kick in the first half. As before, his face gave away nothing. Mac couldn't read him at all. He ended up playing him for the wrong side, and the goal sailed right in.

His halftime sting operation forgotten, Mac slammed his fists against his thighs in frustration.

With the scoreboard reading, Hotspurs 3, Cougars 1, the fans on both sides erupted in an explosion of noisemaking. Half of those watching the game cheered the Hotspur goal while the other half cried out for improved defense from the Cougars.

With the Hotspurs ahead by two goals, the chances of winning the game had decreased considerably.

Still, there were several minutes left to play.

Shortly after the last goal was scored, a collision near the sideline brought a halt in the game. As a Hotspurs defenseman's ankle was looked after, Coach Robertson spoke a few words of encouragement to his players gathered nearby until play resumed.

Jogging back and forth in front of the goal, Mac kept his body alert while his attention was focused on the far end of the field. It looked like Dougie had been revved up by the coach's pep talk. He passed the ball to Jackie at the opposite wing slot, darted toward the backfield, then came straight down the center, ready to receive the ball back.

The Hotspurs' defense expected him to either set up a shot for Jackie or take one himself from that position. Instead, he just

116

kept running forward while Mickey came out of nowhere and took the shot.

*Thwunk!*

The ball sailed into the net at the opposite corner from where it was booted, a nice clean arc that completely missed the Hotspur goalie's desperate attempt to block it.

The scoreboard now read, Hotspurs 3, Cougars 2.

The Hotspurs were obviously surprised by the revived Cougars. This was not the way their games had been going this season. Mac could see that they were having trouble regrouping after Mickey's goal. There were endless tie-ups and tangles on the field. One whistle after another blew as the ball went offside or a drop ball was called.

Both sides were playing a sluggish game. No matter how each tried, they simply couldn't get the ball into an open space long enough to line up a kick.

Mac couldn't restrain himself from calling

out now and then to his teammates at the opposite end of the field. And then, suddenly, as it happened so often, the tide turned and the play was all down at his goal. A tiring Cougars defense let the Hotspurs gain an advantage again and again.

Mac was totally focused. Without a sound coming from his mouth other than the occasional grunt, he was all over the place. He managed to block four successive shots on goal, one after the other, without a ball getting near the net.

When he finally got the chance, he booted the ball to one of the Cougars open at the far corner of the field. At last, the ball began its journey toward the Hotspurs' goal.

The Cougars' fans in the stands went wild. They cheered Mac over and over for the job he had just done at the goal. They then turned their attention to the opposite side of the field, where the action had grown intense.

**15**

Inspired by the change in momentum at the opposite goal, the Cougars' defense had caught fire. Constantly on the move, they opened one passing lane after another. It seemed as though the Hotspurs were always half a beat behind.

Not that they were out of it altogether. Oh, no, Mac could see them getting tougher and tougher in the backfield, that part that was most in his range of vision. They seemed to grow larger as they bore down on the Cougars.

But tougher play also made for mistakes.

119

Moves that had succeeded for the Hotspurs in the first half were no longer as crisp. Timing was off. The ball remained in their control far less than it had earlier.

Jackie was outplaying them better than he had any team all season long. Backed up by a midfielder to his rear and another Cougar forward to his left, he dribbled the ball into good scoring position again and again.

Gradually the Hotspurs defense began to give more attention to the right side of the field, where Jackie held sway. Eventually it seemed as though all eyes were on Jackie and his spectacular display of dribbling.

That left the field pretty clear for Dougie. So when a lane opened up and Jackie managed to get off a beautiful pass across field, Dougie was ready for it. He trapped it with the inside of his left foot, nudged it into position, and took a quick, hard kick in the direction of the goal.

*Thwap!*

The ball rocketed forward, then rose as it approached the goal. The Hotspurs' goalie leaped up to block it, but it glanced off his fingertips — and plopped behind him inside the net.

*Goal!*

The stands went wild. Cheers broke out all over the field as the Cougars converged upon Dougie. They swarmed around him, slapping high fives and tens and hugging him all at the same time.

Rushing in from his position, Mac, too, felt a flush of pleasure at the phenomenal turn-around the team had accomplished in the second half. And Dougie was at the heart of it, no doubt about that. As goalie, Mac had done his part by holding off the Hotspurs' offense — but you don't put points on the scoreboard from the goal area. Glancing up, he could see that the scoreboard looked pretty good right now, reading, Cougars 3, Hotspurs 3.

He caught sight of his parents, huddled together in the late-afternoon chill, waving to him. He nodded back in their direction.

He also saw Jimmy Palumbo. Jimmy was sitting with two girls. Mac flushed slightly when he recognized Deanna. It took him a moment longer to recognize Margie Lewis, the editor of the *Chronicle*. She waved to Billy, who waved back. Guess they must be an item, Mac figured.

A whistle signaling the two-minute warning brought his attention back to the game.

Okay, he thought, just two minutes to hold off the Hotspurs from cracking the targeted area between the goalposts. It's up to me, more than anyone else, to see to that.

Having blocked a near-record number of attempts already, was he up to it? Mac was determined to demonstrate that the answer to that question was a loud and clear "Yes!"

Those final two minutes of the Hotspurs game would long be remembered by fans of both teams. For the players, they were even more memorable.

The two teams dug in with an unbelievable determination. After holding a lead for so much of the game, the Hotspurs were clearly going after one more goal for a win.

Proud that they had come back from such a deficit, the Cougars were equally bent on not giving up the ball for a loss.

And both teams were bone weary. From his position at the goal, Mac could see the drawn lips, matted hair, smudges, spatters, and wear-and-tear of a long hard game almost behind them. More important, he could see clearly what was happening every time the ball got close to his area. That way, he was able to hold off the few attempts made on goal. He seemed to defy the laws of gravity with one stretch or leap after another that kept the ball away from the net.

It looked as though the final whistle would

blow with a mass of players congregated right in front of him, when a pass from one Hotspur to another ricocheted off of Mickey's sharp, bony knee. The ball went sailing in the opposite direction, and the two teams raced down toward the opposite goal.

Seconds were left. The referee was undoubtedly drawing in his breath to exhale through the whistle when a pass from Jackie in Stevie's direction was intercepted by Dougie. Being careful not to get offside, the speedy center had come right up to the line of the penalty area and was in perfect position. He barely tapped the ball with the inside of his shoe, but it went sailing into the net as the whistle blew.

*Score!*

In the most dramatic finish anyone could ask for, the Cougars had pulled it out and won the game: Cougars 4, Hotspurs 3!

"So what do you say about that?" Jimmy Palumbo cried out to Mac. The Cougars' goalie had come speeding toward the bench to join in the celebration with the other members of his team. After showering each other with everything they could find on the bench, they had begun to drift in toward the locker room when the question was asked.

"Fantastic!" Mac called back as he attempted to joined his teammates.

"So, you think *everything* about the game went well?" Jimmy asked significantly.

"We'll find out soon enough," replied Mac.

Mac showered quickly, then joined his parents outside the locker room and received all kinds of praise for his play.

"I don't know what more you could have done to help," said his father. "You played a wonderful game."

"Just like always," added his mother.

**16**

The morning after the game with the Hotspurs, the Williams family piled into their van for a drive to Grandma and Grandpa Williams's house in the next state to celebrate a special birthday: Grandpa's seventieth. There would be a big party, with aunts and uncles and cousins and a stayover at a nearby motel. On the drive up, Mr. Williams told stories about his father and related stories of his own growing up. Mrs. Williams finished the last-minute wrapping of some presents she had bought and also talked about her father-in-law.

Mac asked some questions about his cousins, most of whom were girls. There were a few boys younger than he was, but they were all pretty cool. He was looking forward to seeing them.

The trip went well, the party was a great success, and Mac had a great time at the motel. He ran up and down the corridor to fill up one bucket of ice after another in a race with two of his girl cousins, which he won.

"Boy, you're pretty fast," said Mary Alice, panting.

"It's his soccer training," said Elizabeth. "My folks told me that your folks told them that you're the star of your soccer team at school."

Mac was embarrassed.

"Star? What's a star? A little twinkle in the universe, that's what!" he answered. "Hey, betcha can't make it to the front desk first!" He was off in a flash, trailed by the two girls.

The ride back home on Sunday afternoon was a lot quieter. The weekend had taken his mind off the cartoonist. But now, with Monday morning and a new edition of the *Chronicle* looming in front of him, he couldn't help wondering if Operation Payback had worked.

Luckily it didn't take long to get an answer. By the time the bell had rung at the start of school, kids were lined up for the latest issue of the *Chronicle*. Within minutes, they were chuckling over the latest drawing smack in the center of the paper.

It showed a gorilla wearing Mac's uniform number. The beast was standing on top of the prostrate body of the coach, beating his chest and shouting, "Me take over team! Me know more than you!"

For the first time since the cartoons had started appearing, Mac felt a grin spread over his face. Operation Payback was a success!

Now all he had to do was get a confession from his suspect.

School that day dragged by, and practice wasn't any quicker. But finally both were over. After showering, the Cougars boarded the late-afternoon-activities bus.

The ride would give Mac the perfect opportunity to confront his man. He made sure he was seated right in front of his suspect. Dougie sat with him. When the bus started moving, he turned around to face the person sitting there: Billy Levine. Billy wasn't alone, though. His girlfriend, Margie Lewis, was with him. But Mac didn't care. He wasn't about to let this chance pass by.

"Say, Billy, what'd you think of the cartoon in today's *Chronicle*?" he asked.

Billy shrugged. "I dunno, I guess it was kind of funny. I mean, you were sort of like that at halftime Friday," he mumbled.

"Oh, was I? Well, I'll tell you something really funny."

By now, others on the bus were listening.

"I'll tell you what's funny," Mac repeated. "That whole business at halftime was just an act! And everyone, even the coach, knew it. Except you. And do you know why?"

Billy just blinked.

"Because I wanted to flush out the guy who's been making fun of me in the paper, that's why! And that's just what I did. It is you, isn't it? You're the cartoonist!"

But to his amazement, Billy shook his head. "No, it's not me!" he said angrily. "*I* wouldn't stab a teammate in the back like that. Guess I can't say the same thing for the rest of you." He glared at the other players, many of whom were hanging their heads and shuffling their feet. "Thanks a lot, guys. Nice to know how much you trust me."

Mac was stunned. "But — but it has to be you! No one else would have known about what happened at halftime. And," he added with more conviction, "you were there at the dance, too, when I couldn't talk to Deanna because my mouth was so full. And then there's Margie here —"

Mac glanced at the girl at Billy's side, then did a double take. Margie was staring at him with narrowed eyes, her mouth a thin line of anger.

"How dare you set Billy up like that!" she cried. "That's the meanest thing you've ever done to him — and from what I understand, you've done and said *plenty* of mean things!"

Mac couldn't believe his ears. "What are you talking about?" he asked.

Margie imitated Mac's voice: " 'Do you think the mud on the backside of your uniform will ever come clean?' 'Move it, Billy! Get the lead out!' 'Come on, Billy! Think you could maybe give me a little help here for once?' "

Mac reddened as he recalled saying those very words to Billy — and more besides.

Margie continued, "Billy's told me all

about your never-ending commentary and how his playing factors into it. You're always on his case. So I thought it was time to turn the tables. You'd ridiculed Billy long enough. I wanted you to see how it felt."

"*You?*" Mac and Billy said in the same surprised voice.

Margie sat up straighter. "Yes, *me*. *I'm* the cartoonist."

Dougie broke the awkward silence that followed Margie's confession. "Say, Margie, if you're still looking for more ammo to fire at Mac, I can help you out there," he said in a deadpan voice. "I've been listening to his endless yakking for as long as I can remember."

Jimmy started snickering. Several other boys did, too. At last, Mac and Billy had to join in. Finally even Margie cracked a smile.

"I don't know, Dougie," she said. "Something tells me my drawing days are over."

"Billy, I'm really sorry if anything I said made you mad. I'll be more careful in the future," Mac promised.

"Then I won't have anything to gripe about to Margie," Billy said in a mock complaining voice.

Dougie slapped Mac on the back. "Somehow I don't think you'll have to worry about that," he said. "I mean, come on. Hey, guys, who really thinks Mac will be able to keep his trap shut?"

All eyes swiveled to Mac. He opened his mouth to retort. But then, with a sly grin, he closed it triumphantly.

"Well, what do you know?" Jimmy said. "*Mac's Mouth Made Mute!* Now that's a front page headline for the newspaper!"

"Yeah, it's a real soccer scoop!" Mac added before he could stop himself. As he clapped his hands over his mouth, the others crowed with laughter.

# Matt Christopher®

| | |
|---|---|
| Muhammad Ali | Randy Johnson |
| Lance Armstrong | Michael Jordan |
| Kobe Bryant | Peyton and Eli Manning |
| Jennifer Capriati | Yao Ming |
| Dale Earnhardt Sr. | Shaquille O'Neal |
| Jeff Gordon | Albert Pujols |
| Ken Griffey Jr. | Jackie Robinson |
| Mia Hamm | Alex Rodriguez |
| Tony Hawk | Babe Ruth |
| Ichiro | Curt Schilling |
| LeBron James | Sammy Sosa |
| Derek Jeter | Tiger Woods |

# THE #1 SPORTS SERIES FOR KIDS

# MATT CHRISTOPHER®

## Read them all!

*Previously published as Crackerjack Halfback

All available in paperback from Little, Brown and Company
**Previously published as Pressure Play
***Previously published as Baseball Pals